JUL 2002

W9-DEV-022

3 1524 00355 3940

WITHDRAWN
Woodridge Public Library

Suen,
Anastasia.
E+
Sue   Hamster chase

SEP 0 3 2002	MAY 3 0 2003
SEP 2 1 2002	JUN 2 3 2003
OCT 1 2 2002	
NOV 0 5 2002	AUG 1 1 2003
NOV 1 6 2002	
DEC 1 3 2002	AUG 1 7 2003
MAR 0 7 2003	10-21-03
MAR 3 1 2003	MAR 1 5 2004

WOODRIDGE PUBLIC LIBRARY
3 PLAZA DRIVE
WOODRIDGE, IL 60517-5014
(630) 964-7899

Hamster Chase

A Viking Easy-to-Read

Story by **Anastasia Suen**

Illustrations by **Allan Eitzen**

Based on the characters created by

Ezra Jack Keats

VIKING

WOODRIDGE PUBLIC LIBRARY
3 PLAZA DRIVE
WOODRIDGE, IL 60517-5014
(630) 964-7899

VIKING
Published by the Penguin Group
Penguin Putnam Books for Young Readers, 345 Hudson Street,
New York, New York 10014, U.S.A.
Penguin Books Ltd, 27 Wrights Lane, London W8 5TZ, England
Penguin Books Australia Ltd, Ringwood, Victoria, Australia
Penguin Books Canada Ltd, 10 Alcorn Avenue, Toronto, Ontario, Canada M4V 3B2
Penguin Books (N.Z.) Ltd, 182-190 Wairau Road, Auckland 10, New Zealand

Penguin Books Ltd, Registered Offices: Harmondsworth, Middlesex, England

First published in 2001 by Viking, a division of Penguin Putnam Books for Young Readers.

1 3 5 7 9 10 8 6 4 2

Copyright © Ezra Jack Keats Foundation, 2001
All rights reserved
Text by Anastasia Suen
Illustrations by Allan Eitzen

LIBRARY OF CONGRESS CATALOGING-IN-PUBLICATION DATA
Suen, Anastasia.
Hamster chase / by Anastasia Suen ; illustrated by Allan Eitzen ;
based on the characters of Ezra Jack Keats.
p. cm.
Summary: The class hamster gets loose and it's up to Peter, Amy, and
Archie to find him and lure him back into his cage.
ISBN 0-670-88942-3
[1. Hamsters—Fiction. 2. Schools—Fiction.] I. Eitzen, Allan, ill.
II. Keats, Ezra Jack. III. Title.
PZ7.S94343 Ham 2001
[E]—dc21
00-009703

Printed in Hong Kong
Set in Bookman

Viking® and Easy-to-Read® are registered trademarks of Penguin Putnam Inc.

Without limiting the rights under copyright reserved above, no part of this
publication may be reproduced, stored in or introduced into a retrieval system,
or transmitted, in any form or by any means (electronic, mechanical, photocopying,
recording or otherwise), without the prior written permission of both
the copyright owner and the above publisher of this book.

Reading Level: 1.8

Hamster Chase

Peter took the hamster
out of his cage.
"I'm going to miss you
next week, Mikey," he said.
"Why?" asked Archie.
"It will be Amy's turn
to take care of him," said Peter.

"Peter," said Amy. "I'm . . . ACHOO!"

Mikey jumped out of Peter's hand.

"Mikey!" said Peter. "Come back!"

Mikey ran toward the classroom door.

Peter, Archie, and Amy ran after him.

"Quick!" said Peter, "close the door."

Archie ran past Mikey and . . .

SLAM! . . . closed the door.

Mikey made a left turn
and ran under the computer tables.
"Not the computers," said Peter.
"He'll chew on the wires,"
said Archie.
"Let's pull out the chairs,"
said Amy.
Peter, Archie, and Amy
pulled out the chairs.

"ACHOO!" said Amy.

"There he goes," said Archie.

"Behind the shelf."

"The shelf is too heavy to move,"
said Peter.

"What can we do?" asked Archie.

"What if we make a noise?" said Peter.

"We can tap on the shelf," said Amy.

"Okay," said Archie.

Peter, Archie, and Amy tapped on the shelf.

Tap-tap-tap, tap-tap-tap.

"Come out, little guy," said Peter.

"Don't chew on any wires," said Archie.

Tap-tap-tap, tap-tap-tap.

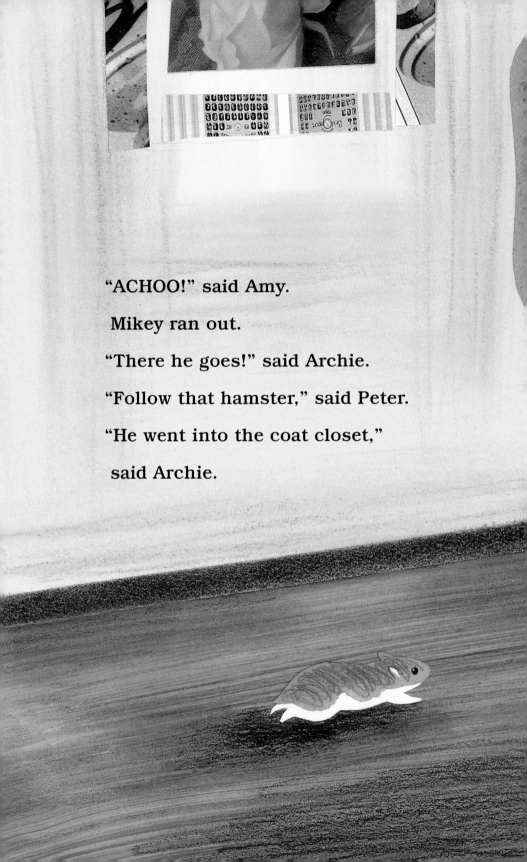

"ACHOO!" said Amy.

Mikey ran out.

"There he goes!" said Archie.

"Follow that hamster," said Peter.

"He went into the coat closet,"

said Archie.

"My lunch is in there!" said Amy.

"Lunch," said Peter.

"That gives me an idea."

"What?" asked Archie.

"Mikey loves to eat," said Peter.

"I don't want him to eat
  my lunch," said Amy.

"We can make a trail," said Peter.

"A trail of food?" asked Archie.

"Yes," said Peter,

"We can make a trail of food

back to Mikey's cage."

"It might work," said Archie.

Peter, Archie, and Amy

went back to Mikey's cage.

"Start with the sunflower seeds,"

said Peter.

"He likes those the best."

One, two, three . . .
Peter put sunflower seeds
in a line on the floor.

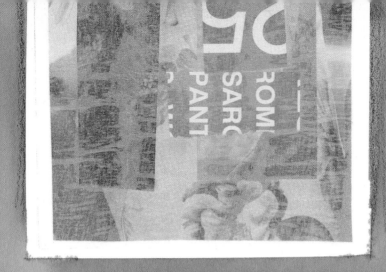

Mikey's nose popped out

of the coat closet.

"It's working!" said Amy.

"Don't sneeze," said Peter.

"How will we get him

back into the cage?" asked Archie.

"We can make stairs
with these books," said Peter.
"Don't make any noise."
Archie, Peter, and Amy
stacked up the books.
One book, two books, three books,
four books, five books, six!
"Hamster stairs!" said Amy.
"Put a few sunflower seeds
on the books, too," said Peter.
Archie and Amy made a trail
of hamster food on the books.

Nibble-nibble, nibble-nibble.

Mikey ate his way out of the closet.

"It's working," said Archie.

Nibble-nibble, nibble-nibble.

Mikey ate his way up to the first book.

"Go up the stairs, little guy,"

said Peter.

Nibble-nibble, nibble-nibble.

"ACHOO!" said Amy.

Mikey jumped into his cage.

Peter closed the door.

"You did it!" said Archie.

"Mikey's fur makes me sneeze,"
said Amy. "Peter, will you
take care of Mikey for me next week?"
"You have a deal," said Peter.

3 1524 00355 3940